Mr RainBoW

Written by Richard Peters

Illustrated by Tayo Olarewaju

Copyright © Richard Peters 2019
Copyright © SJH Publishing 2019

First edition

Published by SJH Publishing
298 Regents Park Road, London N3 2SZ
020 8371 4000
sjhpublishing.org

ISBN 978-1-906670-75-7

Printed in the UK

Dedicated to Charlie and Oscar

Once upon a time, Ollie and Poppy were playing on the slide in their garden.

"Wheeeeeee," said Poppy as she whizzed down as fast as she could.

"Ohhhhhh," sighed Ollie.

"I wish the slide was big enough for both of us so we could have races, don't you Poppy?"

Suddenly they heard a
strange whimpering sound
like someone crying.

Ollie and Poppy went inside
to find out who it was.

"I'm not crying,"
said Mummy.
"I'm making dinner."

Ollie went to check on the fish in the bowl but it was playing not crying.

Poppy went back outside to see if the bumblebees and hedgehogs were the ones crying, but then she noticed something.

"Ollie quick come outside!" she called.

Ollie ran out to the garden to
see Poppy pointing at the grass.
The garden was covered with
colourful puddles.

In the sky they saw
a rainbow crying.

His tears were making the colourful puddles on the grass and he looked sad.

"Mr Rainbow, why are you crying?" asked Ollie.

"Because I've lost a colour and now I'm so sad
I don't know what to do!" Mr Rainbow replied.

"You've lost your colour?" asked Ollie.

"Don't be silly, you're Mr Rainbow,
   you're made of colour," giggled Poppy.

Ollie and Poppy started to sing the rainbow song, pointing at the puddles.

"Red and yellow and pink and green.

Purple and orange and bl..." they stopped suddenly.

"Oh dear," said Ollie. "You HAVE lost a colour – your blue one!"

"Hang on," said Poppy as she ran inside the house. "I have an idea!"

Ollie and Poppy went to their arts and crafts cupboard, which was full of amazing things.

Inside they found a big pot of blue paint and a paint brush!

"Hold still Mr Rainbow, this may tickle a bit," said Ollie.

Ollie and Poppy started to paint the blue back on to Mr Rainbow, but they had to stop.

"We're too little to reach the top," said Poppy, sadly.

"That's not a problem," said Mr Rainbow. "I'll send one of my clouds for you to stand on."

Ollie and Poppy floated up to the top of Mr Rainbow and down the other side, painting his blue stripe as they went.

"That does tickle a bit!"
chuckled Mr Rainbow.

"Finished," cheered Ollie and Poppy.

"Wow, you did it! I'm colourful again!" said Mr Rainbow, smiling down on his new friends.

"I'm going to give you a thank you present," said Mr Rainbow. "Wiggidy squiggidy woo!"

As if by magic, a new super-fast double rainbow slide appeared in the garden.

"Thank you Mr Rainbow,
this is the best slide ever!"
shouted Ollie and Poppy.

Mr Rainbow floated back up into the sky, and Ollie and Poppy spent the rest of the day having races on their new colourful double rainbow slide.